Ivy

Katherine Coville

Illustrated by

Celia Kaspar

Alfred A. Knopf
New York

Visit us on the Web! randomhousekids.com

Educators and librarians, for a variety of teaching tools, visit us at RHTeachersLibrarians.com

Library of Congress Cataloging-in-Publication Data is available upon request.
ISBN 978-0-553-53975-2 (trade) — ISBN 978-0-553-53976-9 (lib. bdg.)
ISBN 978-0-553-53977-6 (ebook)

The text of this book is set in 17-point Cloister.
Jacket design by Nicole Gastonguay
Interior design by Trish Parcell

Printed in the United States of America
March 2017
10 9 8 7 6 5 4 3 2 1

First Edition

Random House Children's Books
supports the First Amendment and celebrates the right to read.

For Cara Joy

Contents

CHAPTER 1

Grandmother's Garden

Once upon a time, in the kingdom of Evermore, there lived a small, round girl named Ivy. Ivy had a way with animals. Beasts and birds were not afraid of her. They let her touch them and feed them and carry them, and though she couldn't understand their languages, she seemed to know what they liked.

Ivy lived with her grandmother, whom the villagers called Meg the Healer. Grandmother was known far and wide as a healer for all the creatures of the farms, fields, and forests, and Ivy was her helper. Ivy had lost her mama and papa when a terrible fever passed over the land, and so she had come to live with Grandmother in the peaceful village of Broomsweep.

Broomsweep was a very clean and orderly place. In fact, that's why it was named Broomsweep. All the cottages were clean. All the streets were clean. Every garden bloomed with flowers planted in straight rows, each flower exactly the same height. No one ever made messes or raised a ruckus. All the children and pets were clean and orderly too. Every morning and every evening, the people of Broomsweep swept their front steps, then they stepped back to admire their nice, clean cottages and nodded in satisfaction.

Everyone except Ivy's grandmother. Her cottage was surrounded by a big, overgrown garden. It was the very last cottage on the outskirts of town, next to the Dark Forest. It was a good place for Grandmother to do her work. But Grandmother did not sweep her front steps twice a day. . . . The truth was that some days she did not sweep them at all! When the people of Broomsweep walked past her cottage, they would sniff and shake their heads in disapproval. Still, if the villagers needed help with their farm animals or pets, they brought them to Grandmother's cottage for her to heal.

Ivy soon learned that even wild animals who needed help knew where to find Grandmother. They would make their way to the cottage and scratch at the back door. And once in a while—in the dark of night, her grandmother told her—something magical, like a dragon or a griffin, might slip through the forest, seeking her help.

"If you should ever see a dragon," Grandmother warned her, "be *very* polite."

So Ivy practiced being polite with all the small animals.

One day, Ivy sat on the back steps holding a chipmunk in her lap while Grandmother examined him. "It's all right, little chippy," Ivy crooned. Her gentle voice and touch were almost as good as Grandmother's for calming a nervous creature, and the chipmunk held still, except for when he sneezed.

"Tell me what you see, Ivy," said Grandmother, whose old eyes didn't work very well.

Ivy held up the wee chipmunk and looked into his face thoughtfully.

"His eyes are clear," said Ivy. "And his ears are nice and pink. But his nose is runny."

"Ah. Just a cold, I think. A little Sneezlewort Potion should help. I'll hold him while you fetch it."

The chipmunk made a chittering noise as Ivy handed him to Grandmother. Ivy chittered back.

She was very good at imitating animal sounds, although she didn't know what she might be saying.

Ivy went to the cupboard in the cottage and read the labels on the potion jars the way Grandmother had taught her. She knew how important it was to get the right potion.

"Take your time," Grandmother always told her, "and check everything twice." So Ivy took her time and read the labels out loud. "Let's see . . . Worry Tonic for the nerves . . . Scratch-the-Itch Powder . . . Claw Polish . . . Limberjuice for stiff joints . . . Sneezlewort for sneezes!" She picked up the jar and checked the label again, then took it to Grandmother.

"Good," said Grandmother. "That's very good."

Ivy smiled happily. She liked to be helpful.

"Now mix three drops with half a spoonful

of oats. Feed him the oats, and send him to bed. He can stay in the empty burrow under the apple tree until he feels better."

Ivy's sharp eyes and small hands made her very good at measuring. She followed all of Grandmother's directions and then set the chipmunk down under the apple tree.

"Go on in, little chipmunk. This hole is for you."

The chipmunk sneezed.

Ivy took a handful of milkweed fluff from her pocket and placed it next to the empty burrow for his bedding. She pushed a clump of the fluff toward him with her finger. The chipmunk sneezed once more. Then, taking the fluff between his teeth, he disappeared down the hole.

Ivy smiled with satisfaction. She drew a bucket of water from the well and made her way through the overgrown berry bushes to a bigger burrow, where an injured fox and his mate crept out to meet her and allowed her to scratch behind their ears. "Good morning, Master Fox, Mistress Fox. How's the tail this morning?" she asked as she offered each of them a little treat from her pocket. The injured fox held still as she removed the bandage from his tail. "You really must be more careful of traps!" she warned him. Then she washed his cuts and gave him a fresh bandage and offered him another treat.

Ivy was just turning back to the cottage, brushing at the dirty paw prints the animals had left on her apron, when she heard voices coming from the road in front of the garden. *Children's* voices. Ivy ducked down and crept silently toward them. She knew all the animals' secret pathways through the garden. She could go from the privet hedge at one end of the garden to the hazel trees all the way at the other end without being seen. This time, she stood up when she came level with the children and said, "Hello!"

Three children stopped and stared at her. "Oh, look!" said the biggest girl. It was Edwina, the shoemaker's daughter. "It's the dirty little girl from the wild woods."

Ivy looked down at her apron. It was smudged with paw prints, little ones from the chipmunk and bigger ones from the foxes. There were bright green grass stains and yellow pollen from the marigolds she had picked that morning. It looked just fine to her.

"Why don't you get rid of all those ugly weeds, Wild Girl?"

Ivy glanced around at the overgrown garden she loved so much. *Ugly?* Grandmother's garden was perfect! She couldn't imagine why anyone would want to change it. "Grandmother uses these plants in her healing potions," she explained, "even the weeds. So we let them all grow. Besides, they're fun to play in. Want to play hide-and-seek? I'll be it."

"My father says this place is a disgrace," said Edwina. "He says the only reason anybody puts up with you two is that your grandmother is a healer. And my mother says I'm not allowed to get dirty, so I'm not allowed to play with you."

"Me neither!" said the girl's little sister, Marta.

"Me neither!" said Peter, who lived next door. Then he stuck out his tongue.

"That's what you always say!" Ivy answered them. She stuck her tongue out at Peter.

"My father says that Broomsweep is the cleanest, most orderly town around—except for *you*," continued Edwina. "Who knows *what's* going on with all those wild animals you keep! Besides, everybody else sweeps their front steps twice a day, and you sweep yours only once."

"Well," said Ivy, "maybe that's because it's *silly* to sweep them twice a day!"

Edwina's eyes grew larger. Her mouth hung open. "I'm telling my papa what you said!"

"Go ahead!" exclaimed Ivy, acting like she didn't care. She heard Grandmother calling her from the front steps and turned. Ivy could see that she was talking to Farmer Higley about his piglet. Ivy made her way through the azalea bushes to the front walkway, leaving the children to stare after her. She took the piglet in her arms and sat down, crooning softly to him until he settled into her lap. "Good little pig," she said, petting him. "Nice piglet."

"Let's have a look," said Grandmother, sitting down next to her on the steps.

"Hey, look at the piggy!" Edwina shouted from the road. She nudged Peter with her elbow.

"You mean the little pink one with the curly tail?" asked Peter, smirking.

"No, I mean the one that's HOLDING him!" yelled Edwina. The three children laughed hysterically at this. They pointed at Ivy and chanted, "Piggy, piggy, piggy!" as they ran away.

"Hmph," said Grandmother. "They seem to think they're being clever."

"I've known donkeys more clever than they are," answered Ivy, as if the teasing didn't matter at all. But her eyes were stinging, and there was a big lump in her throat that she couldn't swallow.

CHAPTER 2

The Queen's Contest

The next morning, Ivy was in the garden feeding worms to an injured robin. It was an icky job, but Ivy didn't mind. The robin had sprained her foot and couldn't hunt for herself.

Ivy dropped one last worm into the robin's beak. She watched as several more robins flew up and away. How Ivy wished she could fly! She paused, imagining for a moment what it would be like to float above the treetops. Then she set the jar of worms on the step and washed her hands in a bucket of water.

As Ivy turned toward the cottage, she heard a small whimper. She looked all about and saw something white and fluffy trying to hide under the lilies. "Poof," said Ivy, "is that you?"

She bent down and scooped up the creature. It was a tiny dog, with large ears and a pink tongue hanging out of its mouth. He looked up at her with big brown eyes. "Back again, Poof?" Ivy exclaimed. "You've been here twice this week already!"

The little dog whimpered once more.

"You know you're not sick, Poof," said Ivy as she tucked him under one arm and went into the cottage. "Grandmother," called Ivy, "Poof is back."

"Let me see him," said Grandmother. She looked the pint-size dog over, then opened his mouth and checked his tongue. "Just as I thought," she said. "You are in perfect health. And your mistress will come looking for you any minute now."

"Can't he stay with us this time?" asked Ivy. "He likes it better here. That's why he keeps coming back."

Grandmother shook her head. "And what would we say to the mayor's wife when she comes to take him home?"

"We could hide him," Ivy offered, scratching under Poof's chin.

"No, my dear, we couldn't."

Ivy heard a knock on the front door. She made a grumpy face. Then she kissed Poof on the top of his head and went to open the door.

A skinny woman in a fancy purple dress glared down at her. It was the grand and haughty Mistress Peevish, the mayor's wife. "Poofie!" she cried. "There's my sweet Poofie-Pie! What a bad boy to run away like that!"

Mistress Peevish reached for Poof. "Give him to me," she demanded. But as she held out her hands, the tiny dog jumped from Ivy's arms and hid under Grandmother's skirts.

"Oops," said Ivy, trying not to laugh.

The mayor's wife saw her smirk. "You wretched little girl! You dropped him on purpose!"

Grandmother smiled sweetly. "I'm sure Ivy didn't mean to cause any trouble. She's really quite a good girl." Grandmother gently lifted Poof out from under her skirts and handed him to the mayor's wife.

"Just look how dirty he is!" declared Mistress Peevish. "He'll need a bath right away." Poof's eyes seemed to bulge as if he were being squeezed too tight. The mayor's wife turned to leave. Then she looked around and gave a sniff.

"This whole place needs cleaning up!" she

pronounced. "This big, overgrown garden is a jungle. There are creatures everywhere, and look! There is *dust* on this doorstep!"

Grandmother just smiled. "I must tend to the animals first. Surely a little dust can wait."

"WAIT?" cried Mistress Peevish. "Haven't you heard?"

"Heard what?" asked Ivy.

"About the queen's contest," replied the mayor's wife importantly. "A rider brought the news just yesterday! The town crier announced it in the village square! King Barney and Queen Bernice have died of the fever."

"That's terrible!" said Grandmother.

"It's very sad, I'm sure," Mistress Peevish answered. "But now we have a new queen! Queen Emmeline! Just think—hardly anyone has laid eyes on her. She's a great mystery. And listen! She's holding a contest for the best town in the kingdom of Evermore. Even now, she's touring the countryside in her royal coach, inspecting each and every town. Broomsweep is to be the very last one, so we must stand out against all the others! They say the new queen will reveal herself when she chooses the winner of the contest. There's to be a royal fair held in the winning town—the *best* town—a fair the like of which has never been seen before!"

"Well, that would be quite an honor," Grandmother responded.

"It certainly would!" continued the mayor's wife. "I just know Broomsweep will be the best town of all. We can have the fair right in our own village square. Only picture it! The mayor and I will meet the queen! Can you imagine? We might even be asked to *sit* with her at the fair. I really should have a new dress. Purple, I think . . ."

At this, Mistress Peevish seemed to run out of words. She stood there with a dreamy look on her face until Poof started to wiggle. Then she gripped him more tightly and said, "You see how it is. We simply *can't* have this big, sloppy mess here anymore. You'll ruin our chances of being named the best town!"

"We wouldn't want that," Grandmother answered, considering the matter. "I need these plants for my medicines and potions, you know. But I'm sure we could tidy things up a bit."

Mistress Peevish frowned. "Or maybe you'll have to grow them somewhere else! And we can't have these animals running wild either—they're dirty and disorderly, and they'll ruin everything! They have to go. Our town is going to be the *best* town, no matter what it takes!"

"But the animals need us! Where would the sick creatures go?" asked Ivy.

"They'll go back to where they came from," said the mayor's wife. "And they'd better be quick about it. The queen will be here in three days. THREE DAYS!"

With that, the grand and haughty Mistress Peevish stepped off the front step, knocking over Ivy's jar of worms. When she looked down and saw them crawling at her feet, she screamed.

"It's all right," Ivy said. "They won't hurt you."

"You terrible child!" cried the mayor's wife. "Fix this place up!" she sputtered to Grandmother. "You've been warned!" And with one last scream at the worms, she turned and ran away.

Ivy and Grandmother looked at each other.

"What are we going to do, Grandmother?" asked Ivy, her chin trembling. "We can't tell the animals to leave!"

"Of course not, my dear," said Grandmother. "But we'll need to do our best to keep them out

of sight for a few days. Now let's get started on the cleanup."

"But how will we ever do it all?" Ivy said, looking around. She felt like giving up before she had even begun.

"We'll tidy up the front of the garden first. I'll get going on the hollyhocks at this end, and you start with the lilies at the other end. We'll work our way toward the middle, and see who gets there first. Save the weeds in a pile for me. Especially the dandelions! Come, let's see how much we can get done before nightfall."

CHAPTER 3

A Guest

Ivy and Grandmother worked all through the day. By the time the sun began to set, everything in the front of the garden was neat and tidy. Ivy had to admit, the flowers looked pretty now that they had been trimmed and weeded. And there was a nice big pile of weeds for Grandmother's potions. Ivy was so tired she couldn't wait to climb into bed.

Night was always a very peaceful time in

Broomsweep. As darkness fell, people put away their brooms and went to bed. They slept with their windows open, for there was never any noise after ten o'clock. Snoring was frowned upon in Broomsweep. Even the crickets stopped their chirping and went to sleep.

That night, the moon shone brightly as Ivy and her grandmother lay sleeping. Grandmother snored just a tiny bit. Ivy was dreaming her favorite dream. It was about flying, as free as the robin. In her dream, she was soaring over the town, higher than the treetops, higher than the church steeple. She shivered with delight as she rode on the wind. Just as she was gliding over the village square, a loud voice cried out in the night.

"Oh no! Oh dear! WHOOPS!"

There was a big, noisy crash behind the house. Ivy's eyes popped open, but she wasn't sure if she was still dreaming.

"OW! Oh, ouch," went the voice. "Oh dear. So sorry. *Terribly* sorry. *Aawk.*"

This time Ivy knew she was awake. So was Grandmother. Ivy looked out the window as Grandmother lit the lamp. She could see the blackberry bushes shaking in the moonlight. She watched, wide-eyed, as Grandmother carefully opened the back door and lifted the lamp. Ivy thought she saw a shape moving in the bushes. It looked like the back end of a giant cat. It had a long tail with a tuft at the end.

"Grandmother!" Ivy gasped. "It's a lion! Be careful!"

"Let's wait and see," Grandmother answered.

As they watched, a huge wing poked out of the bushes. "*Aawk!* Oh, prickers. Oh dear!" cried the voice.

"There's a big bird in there too!" exclaimed Ivy.

"Wait and see," Grandmother said again. She carried the lamp a little closer to the bushes. They could see now where the bird feeder had been knocked down and all the daisies were flattened. The pile of weeds they had saved was scattered all over.

"Oh dear. Stuck," moaned the voice. "Stuck, stuck, stuck."

"Do you need help in there?" called Grandmother.

"Help? Oh yes. Help," the voice said softly. "It's prickers."

Grandmother gave the lamp to Ivy and cautiously started to pull away the blackberry canes. The lion shape wiggled out backward while the tail switched back and forth. But where was the lion's head?

Ivy saw another wing open. The wing was much bigger than she was. Grandmother carefully pulled the last branches away . . . and up popped the biggest bird's head Ivy had ever seen. It looked like a giant eagle but with pointed ears.

The voice came from the bird. It said, "Yes! Oh goodness. Much better. *Aawk.*"

Ivy held the lamp up closer. She saw that the bird's head, wings, and legs were part of the lion's body. It was all one creature! It stood a bit crookedly, leaning toward its left side. Ivy could see that one of the creature's hind legs—the left lion leg—was just a stump. But the beast was still magnificent.

"It talks!" gasped Ivy.

"Yes, of course," said Grandmother. "This is a magical creature. A griffin. It's part eagle and part lion." Ivy marveled at the fantastic beast, from its great head to its glossy feathers to its switching tail. She thought it would be terrifying if not for the warmth in its round golden eyes. Grandmother turned to the creature and said, "How do you do? I am Meg, the local healer, and this is my granddaughter, Ivy. And who are you?"

The griffin was pulling prickers out of its feathers with its beak. He stopped and spit them out. "*Aawk*—so pleased to meet you. So nice, oh so nice. I am Cedric, the three-legged griffin. C. T. L. Griffin at your service—*aawk!*"

"Have you traveled far, Cedric?" asked Grandmother.

"Oh—*aawk*—too far from home. No place like home. But Cedric has no home now. No home," answered the griffin.

"No *home*?" asked Grandmother. "How terrible. Whatever happened?"

"Too terrible. Terribly terrible. So sad," said the griffin. "They—" The griffin stopped. He looked down and gave a little sniff. "They asked me to leave," he whispered.

CHAPTER 4

Work, Work, Work

Grandmother patted the griffin's wing and waited for him to go on. Ivy felt sorry for the grief-stricken creature. She came closer and patted him too. His feathers felt smooth and soft.

The griffin sighed heavily. "I was trouble," said the griffin. "That's what they said. Magical creatures are trouble. Too much trouble for the new queen. The queen's contest, you know.

Got to be the *best* town, they said—
better than Broomsweep, they said. No griffins allowed, they said. Too much fuss. Too
many crash landings. Go away, they said. So
Cedric left. Too bad. Too bad."

"How can we help you?" asked Grandmother.

"Help," replied the griffin. "A healer helps.
Cedric asked all the forest creatures where to
find a healer. Here, they said. So please help,
help, help. It's the leg, you know. Lost it fighting a sea creature. I think it was a crocodile.

Or maybe an octopus. No more leg. No more smooth landings. Make Cedric a *four*-legged griffin again, could you? Then no more crash landings—how I do hate crash landings. And maybe they would take Cedric back—*aawk*. No place like home."

"Oh, my dear griffin," said Grandmother, "I wish that it were in my power to make you four-legged, but my potions cannot help you grow a new leg. Perhaps there's something else I could do to help?"

"Maybe you could stay with us awhile, and we could think about it," offered Ivy.

"Stay?" croaked the griffin. "Cedric stay here, you say—with you, you say? Not too much trouble? Griffins allowed?"

"Not too much trouble at all," Grandmother said, smiling. "We will spread out some straw where the daisies used to be. You can make your nest there."

Ivy's face lit up. "Would you stay, Cedric? Please stay. Grandmother is the best healer. I'm sure she'll think of something to help you!"

"Stay," said the griffin. "Oh yes. Will do. No trouble. Many, many thanks. Most humble thanks."

"Then it's settled," said Grandmother. "You are quite welcome here."

"Oh no he isn't!" someone shouted from behind them. There were the neighbors—Jacob the Baker, his wife, and their son, Peter—standing in their nightshirts at the edge of the garden. They all looked angry in the moonlight.

"We don't want any magical critters around here," called Jacob.

"We don't!" cried Peter.

"They're nothing but trouble!" exclaimed Jacob's wife.

"Trouble!" echoed young Peter, and he stuck out his tongue.

"All this noise when people are trying to sleep!" said Jacob. "What's next?"

The griffin looked upset. "Oh dear, oh dear. So very sorry. Cedric came to see the healer, best good healer, wonderful healer, and—*aawk*—had a bit of an accident. Trouble with landings, you know."

Grandmother patted the griffin again. She smiled sweetly at Jacob the Baker and said, "There, you see? It was just an accident. I'm sure it won't happen again. Why don't we all get some sleep?"

"Mayor Peevish is going to hear about this!" grumbled Jacob as he turned to go.

"And Mistress Peevish too!" said Jacob's wife.

"So there!" sassed Peter, who stuck out his tongue again.

Ivy just smiled sweetly at him, as she had seen Grandmother do, and waved. She followed

Grandmother and helped her carry straw to the back of the garden for the griffin's nest. They made him as comfortable as they could and wished him a good night—or what was left of it.

Ivy returned to bed, but she couldn't sleep. She was much too excited thinking about the griffin. She was a little worried too. Was it true that the new queen would not want a griffin in the best town? If Ivy were queen, *she* would want griffins. Especially this griffin. She wondered how long Cedric would stay with them. She hoped it would be a long, long time. With visions of griffins filling her head, she finally drifted off to sleep.

Meanwhile, far away, on a rocky mountainside, four dark figures crept out of a cave. They were large and smelly, and they poked and pushed and snarled at each other as if they had no manners at all. The figures scratched their backsides and picked their noses, then smiled their horrible smiles and showed their green teeth, and clambered off down the mountain to find some dirty tricks to play. They looked this way and that to see if anyone was around to stop them, but there was no one.

CHAPTER 5

The Buzzing Thing

Morning came, bright and fair. As soon as Ivy opened her eyes, she thought of the griffin in the garden. She could hardly wait to see him in daylight. She dressed quickly and gulped down her breakfast.

But Grandmother said the griffin was still sleeping, and it was never a good idea to wake a sleeping griffin. Even a friendly griffin. So Grandmother sent Ivy outside to start cleaning up the garden. Again.

Ivy looked at the terrible mess that the griffin's crash landing had made. He had skidded from the front of the garden all the way to the back of the cottage, flattening everything in his path. Weeds, flowers, and feathers were scattered everywhere! Ivy groaned. They had worked so hard yesterday, and now the garden was even more of a mess. Then she remembered who had made the mess, and she cheered right up. It was worth all the extra work because now they had a griffin.

Just then, Ivy saw a little white bundle trotting toward the garden at high speed. Poof was back. He dove into the underbrush and disappeared. This time Ivy pretended she hadn't seen a thing.

Ivy bent over and started collecting the scattered weeds in her apron. Something buzzed around her head while she worked. Ivy shooed it away, but it kept coming around. She felt it buzzing at the back of her neck. Ivy swatted at it—and felt a sharp pinch on her hand. "Ow!" she cried. Then something pulled her hair. Ivy turned quickly to see what it was, but it was always buzzing just out of sight.

Ivy froze. She had heard a noise coming from the back of the garden where the griffin was. It was a small "Yip, yip, yip," like a tiny dog would make. Poof! Ivy dropped the plants and ran around the cottage. She turned the corner just in time to see Poof being held by the scruff of his neck in the griffin's beak.

"No, no, Cedric!" Ivy scolded. "Bad griffin! Put him down! CAREFULLY!"

The griffin looked at Ivy with wide eyes. Then he slowly lowered Poof to the ground and let go. "Not breakfast?" croaked the griffin. "Oh dear. Bad griffin. So sorry." He hung his head.

"Definitely not breakfast," said Ivy gently.

"This is Poof. Poof is our special friend. All the creatures in Grandmother's garden are very special. We must protect them."

"Protect?" asked Cedric, raising his head. "Griffins PROTECT!" He puffed out his chest proudly. "Griffins are GUARDIANS, don't you know! C. T. L. Griffin, guardian, at your service—*aawk*."

"That's a great idea, Cedric," said Ivy. "You can be our guardian, and I'll get you some nice oats for breakfast. Do griffins like oats?"

"Griffins like everything," answered Cedric.

By the time Ivy got back with the oats, the griffin was sitting in his nest with Poof stuffed under one wing. "See? Cedric guards the Poof," he said majestically. "Good griffin. Noble griffin."

Poof stuck his head out from under Cedric's wing and yapped. Then he hid underneath it again. Ivy thought he liked hiding under there, so she left him alone. "You be a good guardian, Cedric," said Ivy. "I'll be right here."

For the second time that day, Ivy went to work on the hopeless jumble of uprooted plants in the garden. She had not gotten far when the buzzing thing came back. It circled her head until she felt dizzy. Finally she caught a glimpse of it buzzing by. It seemed like a big bug with wide wings like a dragonfly's.

Ivy was very good at catching dragonflies. She cupped her hands and waited for it to circle again. One quick snatch and she had it. But whatever it was, it did not like being snatched. She felt sharp pinches on her hands, and the buzzing got very loud and angry-sounding.

Ivy opened her thumbs a bit and peeked in. Something spit in her eye! Something else pulled her hair and buzzed around her head. There was more than one! Ivy tried again to sneak a look. This time she kept her face away from her hands as she moved her thumb just a crack. Out popped a tiny head—an exquisitely shaped little *person's* head. It was saying something that Ivy imagined must have been very rude, but she couldn't understand it. She opened her hands all the way in wonder. She had seen pictures of fairies in Grandmother's books, but this creature looked even tinier than a fairy. It was impossibly small and perfect.

The tiny winged person hovered for a minute, shaking its miniature fist at her. Ivy guessed from its wispy yellow dress that it was a girl. As she watched, another of the tiny creatures, a boy dressed in green, landed on Ivy's hand and also shook his fist at her. Then they both buzzed away.

Now that she had looked at the creatures up close, Ivy could see that there were *more* of the tiny winged people buzzing around. She could hardly believe her eyes. She looked over at the griffin. "Did you see that?" she asked.

"Oh yes. Oh dear. It's them," groaned the griffin.

"It's who?" asked Ivy. "Do you *know* them?"

"Oh yes. I'm afraid it's pixies. So sorry."

"Why are you sorry?"

"It's pixies. Terrible pests—*aawk!* Worse than fleas! Must have followed me here from home."

"I think they're cute," chuckled Ivy. No

sooner had she said it than a tiny boy pixie dressed in brown hovered near Ivy's right shoulder. Ivy held very still. She wondered if they could understand what she had said. "I like pixies," she said clearly, hoping they were listening.

"What's this?" asked Grandmother, who had just come out to join them. "Do we have pixies?"

"They came with Cedric, Grandmother," said Ivy. "They pinched me and pulled my hair, but I don't mind."

"Ah. It's true that pixies tend to pinch and pull when they lose their tempers, but they really are lovely little creatures once you understand them. They mostly want attention. If you are friendly to them, they will be friendly to you. They understand everything you say. Here, try this. Say something friendly and polite. Then put your hand out, palm up, and wait."

"How do you do, pixies? Won't you please be friends with me?" asked Ivy. She waited. Soon the girl pixie landed on her open hand. She gave a little curtsy. Ivy heard the faint tinkling of the pixie's laughter, and she laughed too. Ivy noticed that there were more pixies coming to land on her shoulders and arms. She even felt them landing softly on the top of her head. She was covered with pixies.

"Grandmother, look!" Ivy whispered, hardly daring to move.

"Ah, yes. When they all light on you at once, they are giving you their most special greeting," said Grandmother. "It is a great honor. They must like you very much. Perhaps they sense that you are good to small creatures."

"I will be good to them," promised Ivy.

"Just remember about their quick tempers. Never swat them or insult them. And don't try to catch them!"

"I'll remember."

"That's good. Go ahead and enjoy your new friends. Then, as soon as you are ready, we'd better get back to work."

Ivy stood still for several more minutes, talking softly to the pixies, inviting them to make themselves at home in the garden. "There's a hollow in the trunk of the apple tree where you could stay," she told them, "and there's a birdbath you can play in over by the herb garden." After a time, she explained that she had to go back to work. She moved very slowly until they had all flown away.

Then she sighed and went back to work for the third time that morning. She stood the sunflowers up while Grandmother patted dirt around their roots. Soon the big flowers stood in a crooked line, leaning every which way. *Maybe the mayor's wife won't notice,* thought Ivy.

There were still crushed plants everywhere.

Where the sunflowers had fallen, seeds were scattered all over. The zinnias and the marigolds were mashed up into a red-orange smear. And everything was still covered with feathers, leaves, and milkweed fluff. Ivy tried to pick up as many feathers as she could. The faster she grabbed for them, the more they slipped through her fingers. How would she ever get them all?

"WELL!" came a cry behind her. Ivy knew that voice. She dropped her forehead into the palm of her hand and groaned. It was just the voice she didn't want to hear.

CHAPTER 6

The Mayor's Wife

Ivy looked up. There stood the grand and haughty Mistress Peevish in another fancy purple dress. There were feathers sticking to it.

"Well," repeated Mistress Peevish. "And WHAT do we have HERE?"

The griffin raised his head. He looked at Ivy. Ivy looked at Grandmother. Grandmother looked at the mayor's wife.

"We've had a little accident," said Grandmother.

"You've had a disaster," retorted Mistress Peevish.

"*Aawk*—a disaster—*aawk!* Oh dear!" squawked Cedric, looking frightened.

"And what is this . . . this MONSTER doing here?" demanded the mayor's wife, pointing at the griffin.

Cedric's eyes widened. He turned quickly and looked behind him. "Monster? *Aawk*—oh dear! Where is it? Where did it go?"

"Allow me to introduce you to our guest," said Grandmother to the mayor's wife. "This is the griffin. C. T. L. Griffin, to be exact. You may call him Cedric. And what would you like him to call you?" asked Grandmother, smiling sweetly.

"Nothing at all!" snapped the mayor's wife, her face turning red. "He won't be staying that long. And just look at this place! It's a worse mess than it was yesterday! Look at these crooked sunflowers, and these piles of weeds, and all these feathers! And—what is THIS disgusting heap?" she cried, pointing to the griffin's big straw nest. "We'll never win the queen's contest looking like this!

"And this CREATURE," wailed Mistress Peevish. "Everyone knows magical creatures are nothing but trouble! How can we be the cleanest, most orderly town with a magical beast around? Things happen wherever they go! Adventures! Disasters! Too much excitement! People forget to sweep their front steps! What will the queen think of that?" Just then, something began to buzz around the mayor's wife's head. She slapped it away.

"I wouldn't do that if I were you!" Ivy warned her.

"Don't speak to me, you awful child!" said

the mayor's wife. Suddenly, she gave a little jump. "OUCH!" she shrieked. "Something pinched me!"

Ivy knew what had pinched her, but she decided to keep quiet, just as the mayor's wife had told her.

Grandmother kept quiet also.

"You've got BUGS in this garden too!" bellowed the mayor's wife. "This mess! This creature! These bugs! ALL of them have to go!"

Then Grandmother spoke up. "The griffin came to me for help. I can't turn him away. He has no other home to go to. He is welcome here for as long as he needs us. Besides," she added, whispering, "it is very bad luck to turn away a griffin."

Mistress Peevish's face grew even redder. She stamped her foot. "It will be worse luck if the new queen sees him. OUCH! Something pinched me again! What kind of bugs are these, anyway?"

No one answered her.

"Oh, never mind!" she snapped. "Just give me my little Poofie, and I'll be on my way. I know you've got him here somewhere." She craned her neck to look around. "Poofie, come here at once!" she cried, stamping her foot again. "Poofie-Pie!"

Suddenly, the griffin drew himself up to his full height. "I GUARD THE POOF!" he announced, his voice deep and menacing. Poof stuck his head out from beneath Cedric's wing and yapped, then disappeared under it again.

The mayor's wife screamed. "Poofie! He's got my little Poofie! The monster's got my Poofie!"

The griffin opened his beak and spread his huge wings. He made a hissing noise at the mayor's wife. She opened her mouth to scream again, but no sound came out. Instead, she stepped backward and sat right down on the ground. "Cedric, it's all right," said Grandmother. But he went on hissing.

Ivy's thoughts raced. She wanted Poof to stay, but she saw Grandmother looking at her. She knew what Grandmother would want her to do.

"Cedric," said Ivy, "you can stop guarding Poof. He's not in any danger. He just has to go home now."

Still hissing, the griffin turned to Ivy. "I GUARD THE POOF! GOOD GRIFFIN! NOBLE GRIFFIN!" he proclaimed more loudly. His huge wings flapped, and the feathers on his head stuck out. Ivy felt a little bit afraid.

Grandmother spoke soothing words to calm him down. The griffin settled back into his nest, still covering Poof with his wing. But when Grandmother came closer, he opened his beak and looked scary.

Finally Grandmother turned to the mayor's wife. She helped her up. Then she put her arm around her. "Now don't you worry, dear. Just give us some time to talk to Cedric. I'm sure we can work this out. And Poof will be just fine."

Mistress Peevish backed away. "This is all your fault! I told you magical creatures were nothing but trouble! And now look what's happened! The mayor will have something to say about this!"

The buzzing began around her head again, and she waved her arms in the air. "OUCH!" she howled. "Poofie!" she pleaded. "Come! Come, Poofie, it's time for your bath—OUCH!"

Poof slowly crept out from under the griffin's wing and looked at Mistress Peevish. He turned and looked at Cedric. Then he dove back under the griffin's wing. The mayor's wife stamped one foot, then the other. Then she tried to stamp both feet at the same time and ended up hopping up and down, still waving her arms in the air.

"I can't stand this another minute!" she spluttered. "I'm going home! But don't think this is the end of it. I'll be back tomorrow with help!

OUCH! There are only two days left! TWO DAYS! And if you don't fix this mess and get rid of that horrible beast—*OUCH!*—someone will do it for you! Just wait and see!"

And with that, the proud and haughty Mistress Peevish turned and ran away.

CHAPTER 7

A Little to the Left!

Ivy and Grandmother watched the mayor's wife run up the road.

"She sure is mad," said Ivy.

"She is a woman of deep feelings," agreed Grandmother.

"I guess this means we have to go back to work," said Ivy with a heavy sigh.

"Yes. There is much to do, and very little time," said Grandmother. "But we'll do our best, won't we?"

"Yes, Grandmother. But what about Cedric?" asked Ivy. "The mayor's wife doesn't like him very much."

"Nonsense," answered Grandmother. "They just need to get to know each other better. It will all work out."

Throughout that afternoon, Ivy and Grandmother worked away. The pixies were not very helpful, but they kept Ivy company and made her laugh, tickling her and doing acrobatics in midair. Ivy picked up the plants that the griffin had knocked down the night before. She saved the ones Grandmother could use and sorted them into separate piles. Grandmother spent the afternoon cooking up potions from the uprooted plants. Sometimes she called Ivy in to help with the measuring.

Cedric wove the leftover plants into his nest. He built the sides so high that Poof was completely hidden. Then Ivy asked him to help straighten up the sunflowers. She stood back and directed him while he tilted each plant until it looked just right, and she patted more soil up around the roots to hold them in place.

They worked late into the afternoon. Finally, the mess from the griffin's crash landing was cleaned up—except for a lot of loose feathers. There was a long bare patch in the garden where the plants used to be, but that couldn't be helped. Grandmother nodded and said their work was done.

"Now, Cedric," said Grandmother, "we must think of a way to improve your landings. We can't have you crashing every time you come down to earth."

"No crashing—*aawk*," said the griffin. "No more crashing. Good, good, very good."

"How is your stump, Cedric?" asked Ivy thoughtfully. "I mean where the crocodile got you. Does it still pain you?"

"Not so bad. Not so very bad. It will do," answered Cedric. "After the croc got Cedric—*aawk*—or maybe it was an octopus, there was a good child—*aawk*—brave child, who found Cedric, took care of Cedric, brought Cedric food. Rolfe, it was. Good child! Brave child!"

"Then what happened?" coaxed Ivy.

Cedric looked to the right, then to the left, and then down at his front feet. Ivy thought he wasn't going to answer her, but then she heard him say softly, "Then Cedric tried to fly. It was crashing into this! Crashing into that! Dirt flying! Things broken! Things flattened! So much trouble! *Too* much trouble, that's what villagers said. Many villagers. Angry villagers. Get out! they said. Then goodbye, home. Goodbye, Rolfe. Goodbye."

Ivy stroked the griffin's back where the feathers met the fur. She thought she detected a single tear in Cedric's eye, and it matched the one in her own, and the one in Grandmother's. Then Ivy thought of something and brightened. "But just think," she said, "if they hadn't sent you away, you would never have found *us!*"

"Oh, yes!" cried the griffin, perking up. "And finding Poof! Now if only Cedric could stop crash-landing."

"Then let's get right to work!" said Grandmother, with her hands on her hips.

"But—*aawk*—how?" asked Cedric worriedly.

"You must show me how you land," said Grandmother. "Perhaps if I watch closely, I can see what the problem is."

"Oh dear," fussed the griffin. "More crashing. Oh dear, oh dear."

"You must be brave, Cedric," said Grandmother. "It's the only way."

"But I guard the Poof!" said the griffin.

"It's all right," said Ivy. "I'll watch over him for you. Here, Poof." Poof jumped out of the nest and ran straight to Ivy. The griffin did not object, so Ivy picked up Poof and followed Grandmother around the house to the road in front. The griffin hopped reluctantly along behind them, moaning softly.

"This will make a good place to land," said Grandmother. "Do you think you can aim for the road?"

"Aim is not so good anymore. Not good at all. Balance is off," replied the griffin, shaking his head sadly.

"Well, then we shall have to work on that too," declared Grandmother. "I shall stand on a spot in the road, and when you are ready to land, keep your eyes on me. I'll point if you need to go left or right."

"Oh dear. Oh dear," moaned the griffin. "Not good. Not

such a good idea . . . but Cedric will try—
aawk. Brave griffin! Mighty griffin!"

Cedric opened his wings and took off into
the sky. He circled above them while Grandmother stood in the middle of the road. Ivy
and Poof stood on the front steps to watch as
the griffin swooped down, aiming shakily for
the road.

"Ooohhhh dear!" wailed Cedric as the road
got closer.

His legs were just a few feet from the ground when panic overtook him. *"Aawwwwwwwwwk!"* He tried to lift up again, but he was going too fast. Cedric's hind foot smacked awkwardly on the ground, and the rest of him just kept going, end over end, until he was a rolling ball of feathers, fur, and flapping wings . . . heading straight for Grandmother!

But Grandmother stood firm. "A little to the left!" she called, pointing away from the garden.

"To the left! To the LEFT!" Ivy shouted from the steps while Poof yapped excitedly.

"Ooohhhh no," cried the griffin as he tumbled to the right. "Oh dear, oh dear! WHOOPS!" he squawked, mowing down yet another row of plants and crashing up against the cottage.

CHAPTER 8

Golden

"Oh, ouch," said the griffin. "Oh dear. So sorry. So terribly sorry. *Aawk*—bad griffin has done it again." Poof ran over to the griffin and licked his face.

Ivy rushed after him. "Talk to me, Cedric! Are you all right?"

"Oh yes. Oh dear. Maybe so." He choked and tried to sort himself out as the dust began to settle.

"Don't you worry about this," said Grandmother. "This was my fault. You did beautifully. You only lost your nerve a bit at the end is all, but we can work on that. Now dust yourself off and we'll try it again."

"Must do it again, must we?" moaned Cedric.

"Yes," answered Grandmother. "We must. This time I want you to glide down slowly and easily, just as if you were coming to rest in a nice, soft nest."

"But I will crash because of having only three legs."

"No, you won't," Ivy reassured him. "Just imagine you are an eagle. An eagle lands on only two legs—*you* have one extra!"

"Extra?" said the griffin hopefully.

"Why, yes," Grandmother said to Ivy. "That's a fine idea." Then she turned to Cedric and stroked his wing, saying, "You are part eagle yourself. When the ground starts getting close, I want you to look at me and think like an eagle. Can you do that?"

"Think like an eagle," repeated the griffin. "Must practice—*aawk!*"

"Yes, Cedric dear," said Grandmother. "Now up you go. Let's begin again."

All through the evening, the griffin practiced landing like an eagle. The first two tries went badly, but at least he managed to miss the garden. By the third try, a crowd had started to gather. Jacob the Baker and his wife and Peter stood on their front steps, watching with their arms folded and angry looks on their faces. Bess the Candlemaker was watching too, from a safe distance, and so were James the Shoemaker and his daughters.

They all watched as the griffin went up into the air. They all watched as he came back down. They all shook their heads as he scrambled to land in a cloud of dust.

Each time the dust settled, Cedric would shake himself off and try again. Ivy and Grandmother cheered him on. On the sixth try, the griffin thought so hard about being an eagle that he nearly forgot to panic. Things went much better after that.

On his seventh and eighth tries, he approached the ground more slowly. And on his ninth try, he hardly skidded at all, but he was tired and discouraged.

"Oh, ouch," moaned the griffin, covering his head with one wing. "Maybe enough tries for today."

"But, Cedric!" cried Ivy. "You can't give up now! You're so close! Won't you please try one more time? Pleeease?"

Cedric sighed heavily, and sighed again. Then he shook the dust from his feathers and said, "Will do my best!" He leaped into the air and began to circle. Ivy held Poof tightly as

Cedric began to spiral downward. She watched the griffin line up with the lane and glide in slowly . . . lower . . . lower. Ivy held her breath as his front eagle claws reached for the ground. He hovered there for a moment, his wings flapping to hold him upright, then touched down his rear lion foot and found his balance, right in front of Grandmother. Cedric folded his wings gracefully as a look of surprise and joy came over him.

"Woo-hoo!" Ivy cheered.

"Woo-hoo!" Cedric cried. Ivy clapped her hands and jumped up and down. Cedric took a bow. "Good griffin! Clever griffin!" he said.

"Yes," agreed Ivy. "Graceful griffin too!"

"Well done," said Grandmother, stroking his broad back.

Everyone came closer, staring at the griffin. Only Jacob was still looking around for some trouble. "Aha!" he said. "Look at that! Now he's done it!"

"Done what?" asked Ivy.

"There!" he replied, pointing to Grandmother's house. The whole cottage was covered with a thick coating of dirt. The clouds of dust the griffin had raised with his landings had settled over everything. The roof was covered with dust. The walls were covered with dust. The windows were covered with dust.

"And look!" yelled Peter, pointing at the garden. Every leaf and flower in the garden was covered with dust too. The villagers gasped in horror. The shoemaker's children, Edwina and Marta, snickered.

"Messy, messy, messy," they chanted, just loudly enough for Ivy to hear.

Ivy looked away and pretended she hadn't heard them, but her throat tightened up. Why did they have to be so mean? She tried to think of something to say back to them, but as she watched Grandmother smiling and talking softly to the angry villagers, she knew Grandmother would want her to do the same. Ivy gazed at the dust-covered cottage and garden. The sun was setting and the orange light on the dust made everything look golden. "Look at that," said Ivy, smiling. "We have a cottage made of gold and a garden of golden flowers. I think it's pretty."

"It's just dirt," said Bess the Candlemaker. "You'll never be able to sweep all that up. Never. And the new queen is coming in two days."

Grandmother shook the dust from a few leaves while Ivy blew dirt from a flower. It was clear it would take a long time to clean up . . . again.

"Perhaps it will rain," said Grandmother brightly. "You never know."

"I know that magical critters are nothing but trouble," announced James the Shoemaker, "and this just proves it! He's got to go!"

"Oh dear," said Cedric. "Oh dear, oh dear." The big griffin got behind Ivy and ducked his head, trying to make himself very small and hoping no one would notice him.

"The griffin's home is with us, for as long as he needs one," answered Grandmother firmly. "But don't you worry about the queen. I'm sure it will all work out."

James the Shoemaker had just opened his mouth to speak when something began buzzing around his head. He swatted it.

"You shouldn't do that," cautioned Ivy. The shoemaker paid no attention. He just kept swatting.

"OW!" he hollered. "Something pinched me!"

Soon there was buzzing around the heads of

all the neighbors. They began to slap at the air. Before long, all of them were shouting "OW!" and "OUCH!" Some began running away.

"Just you wait!" threatened Jacob the Baker. "I've been to see Mayor Peevish! He's coming here tomorrow with the whole town council! He'll fix you!" Then Jacob and his family raced home.

The last of the daylight was fading. "My," said Grandmother, "what a busy day this has been. And tomorrow we shall have to be up early to get ready for our visitors. Imagine! The mayor and the whole town council coming to call. Perhaps we should invite them in for tea."

Grandmother looked over the blanket of dust and the damage done to the garden. She yawned tiredly. "This," she said, "will have to be continued in the morning. What we all need first is a good night's sleep."

CHAPTER 9

No Place to Rest

Not so far away, on a moonlit road, four dark figures prowled through the shadows. They scratched their backsides, picked their noses, and snorted with glee. Along their way they had frightened a herd of deer, played the drums on a box turtle's shell, and chased a bear. Now they were filling a badger's hole with dirt and stones. They were trolls, nasty as they could be. Nobody liked them, and they didn't care. They just smiled their horrible smiles and showed their green teeth and looked for more mean tricks to play.

And so they traveled, uphill and down, right to the outskirts of the village of Broomsweep. There they sneaked around in the darkest shadows, watching and waiting to see where they could cause the most trouble.

It was another peaceful night in Broomsweep. The crickets had gone to sleep, and quiet filled the air. The moon shone silver on Grandmother's dusty cottage. Inside, Grandmother snored just a little bit, and Ivy was dreaming her favorite dream. She was flying over the village, higher than the treetops. She was gliding over the village square. This time she saw people down below. They looked very small.

She was trying to look closer and see their faces . . .

When suddenly there was a big noise:

"AH-AH-AH-*CHOOO!*"

Ivy's eyes popped open just in time to see a flash of light behind the cottage. She knew this was not part of her dream. There was a loud knock on the back door, and then Ivy heard it again:

"AH-AH-AH-*CHOOO!*"

There was another flash of light from outside as Grandmother lit the lantern and hurried to open the door. Through the open doorway, Ivy could see a small fire on the ground. She could also see a pair of large, lizard-like feet stamping the fire out.

"Good evening, dragon," said Grandmother.

At this, Ivy had to stick her head out the door and look. There really was a dragon in their own backyard! He seemed a bit small for a dragon, but he was a real dragon all the same. His scales shone bright green in the lantern's light.

"Do forgive be," he was saying, "but I would like very buch to speak to the healer."

"I am Meg the Healer," said Grandmother. "That's a terrible sneeze you have there, my dear. Are you feverish?"

"I thik so," answered the dragon. "I thik I have a code."

Over in the griffin's nest, Poof was yapping excitedly. Cedric stuck his head up and said, "Who goes there—*aawk*?"

"Oh, excuse be for disturbig you. Balthazar is by nabe. How do you do? I didit bean to wake you, it's just that I have this code."

With that, he gave another sneeze, shooting flames out both nostrils and setting fire to a nearby rosebush. Ivy quickly grabbed the water bucket and put out the fire.

"The first thing we must do is find you a safe place to rest," said Grandmother. "Ivy, please

the stream. He can stay under the big weeping willow tree near the water's edge and aim his sneezes at the stream. I must prepare a potion."

Ivy felt a little nervous. She never imagined that she would be so close to a real dragon, even a small one. She wondered if he would sneeze on her by accident.

"Dote worry," said the dragon, as if he were reading her thoughts. "If I have to sdeeze, I'll sdeeze in the other direction."

"That's very kind of you, I'm sure," replied Ivy politely. She remembered Grandmother telling her about dragons and to be very polite to them. "My name is Ivy," she said. "Won't you please come this way?"

Ivy led Balthazar down the path to the stream and over to the weeping willow tree. Its soft branches hung down to the ground like a curtain. Ivy pulled the branches aside and showed the dragon how they made a little room around the trunk.

"Ahhh. Thak you," said the dragon. "This will be fine. I've had no place to rest since they bade be leave by cave. That's why I caught a code."

"Someone made you leave your cave?" asked Ivy. "Why?"

"They didit want any bagical creatures. Too buch trouble, they said. Too disorderly," answered Balthazar. "All I did was blast by flabing breath dowd the mountaidside, but they wouldit listen. They kept goig on about the dew queen. The dew queen this. The dew queen that. And a contest of sub sort. I thought they were all very disrespectful. I left, right then and there. I'll let them worry about the trolls, I said. It wote be by fault if anythig happens."

"The trolls?" asked Ivy.

"Yes. You know. Big, hairy creatures with ruddy doses. Always misbehavig. Very rude. They live in the cave below bine, but they are afraid of my flabe, so I always kept them from causig any trouble. But dow they are probably runnig wild."

"How terrible!" exclaimed Ivy.

"Yes," the dragon agreed. Then he poked his head out of the curtain of hanging branches and sneezed—"AH-AH-AH-*CHOOO*!"—shooting flames right into the stream. There was a loud sizzling sound, and a cloud of steam rose into the night air.

"Bless you!" said Ivy.

"Thak you," said the dragon.

"So you've been banished from your home too?"

"Yes. I'b quite without a hobe. It is a hard thig to bear when you are as old as I ab."

"How old are you?" asked Ivy. Looking more closely at him in the lamplight, she could see that some of the green scales had turned silver at the edges. Then she thought it might not be polite to ask about the dragon's age. "I'm sorry," she said. "I shouldn't have asked."

"Oh, it's quite all right. I will be three hudred years old this winter."

"You must be very wise after having lived so long."

"Oh yes. You can ask be anythig. I'b very helpful."

Ivy smiled. "Hmm. We do have a problem," she began. "Maybe you could help us."

CHAPTER 10

Peter

"Yes?" replied the dragon. "Go ahead. You can tell be."

"Well, to start, everybody in town is angry with us. They don't understand us at all."

"Ah. It sounds as if you need sub freds."

"Freds?" asked Ivy.

"Yes. You know. People who like you, who will stick up for you."

"Oh, you mean *friends?*"

"Yes, freds. That's what I said," replied the dragon. "You deed to make freds with these people. Freds will accept you the way you are. Share subthig with them. Just start with one person. One at a tibe. That's by advice."

Ivy thought about this for a minute. She tried to imagine making friends with any of the children who called her names, but she couldn't. She thanked the dragon anyway.

Ivy stayed to keep Balthazar company until Grandmother arrived with her potion a little while later. By then Ivy was yawning. She was very, very tired. Grandmother yawned too as she gave the dragon a bucket of the superstrength Sneezlewort Potion she had prepared. They wished the dragon a good night and followed the path back up to the cottage. As they walked, Ivy told Grandmother the dragon's story.

"It's a good thing he came here," said Grandmother. "He can stay with us now."

"Does that mean we're going to be in even more trouble?" asked Ivy.

"I expect so," said Grandmother, "but let's give it a little time. I'm sure we can work something out."

Ivy wondered how Grandmother could be so sure, but she decided not to ask.

After all the night's excitement, Ivy and Grandmother nearly overslept. Ivy rushed through breakfast. She hurried to take care of all the creatures. She gave each of them fresh food and water and bedding.

She checked on the fox whose tail had been caught in a trap. She washed his cuts and changed his bandage again. She gave him and his mate each a little treat and scratched behind their ears.

She petted a beaver who had a beesting on his nose and put a little of Grandmother's Anti-sting Potion on him.

The chipmunk's sneeze had improved and he wanted to play, but Ivy knew she had to hurry. Mayor Peevish and the whole town council would be coming today, and Ivy worried that the mess would never be cleaned up in time. But Grandmother said they could only do their best, so Ivy grabbed a broom and started to sweep while Grandmother made up more potion for the dragon.

Soon there was a buzzing around Ivy's head. She laughed and said hello to the pixies. Some of them sat on her head and shoulders as she worked. She was glad the pixies liked her, even though they tickled.

Ivy had barely finished sweeping the front steps when she noticed Peter spying on her from the bushes. She frowned. Why should she be nice to him when he called her names and stuck out his tongue all the time? Ivy got mad even thinking about it. She had had enough of Peter's nastiness. Just to see what would happen, she pointed to his hiding place in the bushes and said, "Get him, pixies! Get him!"

No sooner were the words out of her mouth than a swarm of pixies followed Ivy's outstretched arm straight toward Peter. They began buzzing around his head, pulling his hair, and pinching him. Peter jumped from the bushes, slapping his neck and then his arms. "OW!" he yelped, swatting at the air. "OUCH!" The buzzing rose to a fever pitch, and the pinching got worse and worse. Peter looked as if he might cry.

Suddenly Ivy felt sorry for him. What had she done? She remembered what Balthazar had said the night before about sharing something to make a friend. The pixie attack wasn't going to make Peter her friend!

"Stop, pixies, please stop!" Ivy commanded, but the pixies continued to buzz angrily around Peter. He was going to have to make friends with them the same way she had.

"Peter!" she said. "I can help you! I have something special to show you. Do you want to see?"

"Anything! Just get rid of these bugs!" he bawled.

First Ivy took both of his hands tightly in hers so he would stop swatting. Peter was so surprised that he stopped fussing and looked into her face as if he had never seen her before.

"Listen, Peter," Ivy said, "they're not bugs. They're wonderful little people with wings. They're pixies. If you can make friends with them, they'll stop pinching you."

"I don't believe you!" said Peter, sniffling.

"They understand everything you say. Say something nice to them. Say 'I like pixies.'"

"What?"

"Say 'I like pixies' or 'Magical creatures are nice.' Just say something friendly."

"This is stupid," said Peter.

"Trust me!" insisted Ivy.

"Oh, all right," grumbled Peter. "Pixies are nice."

"Good. Now hold out your hand like this," said Ivy. "Hold it very still. And just keep talking!"

"I like pixies. Pixies are nice," Peter droned. Something whizzed past his head, and he started to look around. "I wish I could see one," he said. As soon as Peter said the words, a tiny pixie landed on his open hand and took a bow. Peter's face lit up. "This is a pixie?" Peter asked in astonishment. "This is the tiniest person I've ever seen! It's not a bug after all!" Smiling broadly, he brought his hand a little closer to his face to see the pixie more clearly.

"I *do* like pixies!" he said quietly. "They are wonderful, aren't they?"

"Just don't try to grab them," Ivy warned, "or they won't be friendly anymore."

"Will they come home with me?"

"I don't know. You'll have to ask them. Be polite."

Peter spoke to the pixies more nicely than Ivy had ever heard him speak to anyone before. She hoped he would stay nice now and stop teasing her the way he usually did.

"If you want," Ivy said cautiously, "I'll introduce you to the griffin. And I'll tell you a secret: we have a dragon now too! He has a cold and he sneezes fire."

"I want to see," said Peter, his eyes going wide.

"I can't take you right now," Ivy said. "But maybe later. Grandmother and I have to clean up the whole garden and the cottage before the mayor comes." She took the edge of her apron and began wiping dust off an azalea plant, one leaf at a time.

Peter tried to say something, but it looked as if his mouth might break. Finally the word came out: "P-please? Please may I see your dragon?"

Ivy was so surprised she dropped her apron. She had never heard Peter say "please" before.

"I guess I can take a little break," she chuckled. "Come on, then. Just remember, you must always be *very* polite to dragons." Ivy led Peter around the house and down the path to the weeping willow tree.

CHAPTER 11

Deep Trouble

In the village square, a crowd was forming.
People were carrying shovels and rakes and
brooms. At the center of the crowd were the
ten members of the town council. At the center
of the town council stood the mayor, the
Honorable Dudley Peevish. And directly behind the mayor stood his wife.

"Now tell them that this just won't do!"
hissed Mistress Peevish to the mayor, poking
him in the ribs.

"Umm . . . this just won't do," said Mayor Peevish to the town council.

The members of the town council said to the crowd, "This just won't do!"

"Tell them that their terrible mess must be cleaned up!" insisted the mayor's wife.

"The . . . uh . . . terrible mess must be cleaned up," said the mayor.

"Tell them the magical creature has *got* to go!" demanded the mayor's wife. "Say that he's upsetting everyone! Tell them the beast stole my Poofie-Pie! Tell them!"

The mayor repeated everything she told him.

"Now let's go!" commanded his wife.

"Now let's go!" echoed the mayor. Mistress Peevish poked him in the ribs again, and he began to march down the road, with her right behind him. The town council marched after them.

They all came to a stop in front of Grandmother's cottage. The mayor's wife stuck her elbow in the mayor's side. "H-h-hello?" called the mayor. There was a short silence. "There's no one home," said the mayor. "I guess we'd better leave."

"Oh, no you don't," declared the grand and haughty Mistress Peevish, and she marched right up to the front door and banged on it.

Down at the stream, Ivy and Peter were having a lovely visit with Balthazar and Cedric, and Poof had joined them. The dragon and the griffin were taking turns telling the children stories. Ivy liked the story of the search for the hornless unicorn. Peter's favorite was the story of the dragon and the three blind knights.

At first Peter had been a little afraid to get close to the magical beasts. They were the most magnificent creatures he had ever seen, but they were very friendly and pleasant to him. They called him Master Peter, which made him feel quite grown-up.

When Ivy finally said she had to go back to work, Peter was sorry to leave. "Can I come and visit again?" he asked as they walked back up the pathway to the cottage.

"You can if you're always as nice as you are now," said Ivy.

Peter looked a little embarrassed. "I'll try to be," he promised.

Ivy smiled happily and said, "All right, then."

It was only when they rounded the corner of the cottage that they saw the people gathered in front of it. Ivy saw the mayor's wife standing on the doorstep, banging on the door. Behind her stood the mayor and the whole town council and the crowd of villagers, shaking their shovels and rakes and brooms. She thought she and Grandmother must be in deep trouble, and her throat tightened. What should she do?

Just then, Grandmother opened the door. She was wearing her work apron and holding a jar of potion in her hand. "Oh, you've come!" said Grandmother brightly. "I was just fixing up some medicine for the dragon. He has such a terrible cold."

Ivy made her way to the door and quietly slipped in to stand by Grandmother's side.

"Dragon? What dragon?" demanded Mistress Peevish, who was almost turning green.

"Oh, you haven't met him yet. He just arrived last night," said Grandmother, smiling sweetly. "I'm sure you'll like him when you get to know him. He's very well mannered."

"Why, you . . . you . . . you can't do this!" spluttered the mayor's wife, shaking her fist. She grabbed the mayor by the collar and pulled him up to the doorstep. "Tell her! Tell her she can't have a dragon! Not with the new queen coming tomorrow to judge our town! Tell her all the magical creatures have to go!"

"Uh . . . um . . . I guess the magical creatures had better go," mumbled Mayor Peevish.

"Nonsense!" said Grandmother. "They'll be just fine here. I couldn't think of sending them away when they came to me for help. Perhaps you'd like to meet them? They're really very charming."

"No, he wouldn't like to meet them!" snarled Mistress Peevish. "And if you won't tell them to leave, the mayor will! Won't you?" she said to the mayor, poking him in the ribs again.

The mayor looked up at his wife's angry face. He looked at Grandmother smiling sweetly. He appeared as though he would like to go hide somewhere, but he couldn't. "Well . . . um," he said. "I guess we'd better not see any magical creatures around here, that's all I can say. Isn't that right, dear?" he asked his wife.

"We'd better not," she threatened, "or we'll run them out of town ourselves!"

"Yes," said all the town councilors, "we'll run them out of town!"

"Run them out of town!" yelled the crowd. "Run them out of town!" And they shook their shovels and rakes and brooms.

CHAPTER 12

Wha-ha-ha-ha!

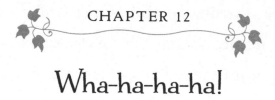

Back in the village square, four dark figures crept out of the shadows. The trolls had arrived in Broomsweep, and they were up to no good.

The biggest troll grunted to the others. The grunt meant, "Drat! There are no humans here. Where has everyone gone?"

A short, fat troll grunted back to him. His grunt meant, "Oh bother! We came all this way for nothing!"

Suddenly a tall, thin troll gave an excited grunt, which meant, "I smell humans! Lots of them! Let's follow the scent!"

The last troll sniffed the air with his big nose and grunted back, meaning, "It's humans, all right! Let us go and find them!"

The trolls sneaked down the side of the cobblestone street, staying in the shadows. They snuffled and snorted, following the human scent past the village square, down the main street, to the other side of town. Closer and closer to Grandmother's cottage.

Back on the main road into town, a golden coach with two snow-white horses made its way uphill and down, heading toward the Broomsweep village square. It was the queen's coach, and it was coming to Broomsweep a day early.

The coach slowed as it entered the village. Its windows seemed to look out at the village like big, dark eyes. Slowly the coach rolled past prim rows of houses without a speck of dirt. Their windows sparkled. Their gardens were trimmed and weeded, and their front steps were all swept. Each house looked like the next, scrubbed clean and perfect, but no one seemed to be home.

The golden coach came to a stop in the middle of the village square, but the village square was empty. Far down the street there was a noise. It was the roar of many voices crying out at once. The golden coach followed the noise down the street to the edge of town, where it came upon a crowd of yelling people in front of a small cottage. And there the coach stopped.

No one noticed.

Standing on Grandmother's front steps, Mistress Peevish was still doing her best to inflame the crowd. "We'll run them out of town ourselves!" she cried, and the crowd repeated, "Out of town! Out of town!"

"And this mess must be cleaned up! All of it!" bellowed the mayor's wife.

"Clean the mess! Clean the mess!" the crowd chanted, waving their shovels and rakes and brooms in the air.

Deep in the shadows of Grandmother's hazel trees, the trolls were lurking. They'd found the humans at last! And what a delicious assortment of humans it was. The biggest troll grunted to the others, meaning, "I'm going for the noisy one on the steps!" And with that, he leaped out of the shadows, bellowing, "Wha-ha-ha-ha!" and snatched up the mayor's wife. Tucking her under one arm like a ball, he charged through the crowd and on down the road.

The crowd scattered. "Trolls!" they screamed. "Trolls!" Only then did anyone notice the royal coach with its two snow-white horses stopped on the far side of the road. The two coachmen looked straight ahead and did not say a word.

"It's the queen!" someone called out. "It's the new queen!"

Everyone gasped in dismay. The mayor's wife had just been snatched by a troll. Now here was the queen a day early, right in front of the messiest place ever seen in the village of Broomsweep!

Before anyone could think of what to do, the big troll circled back, and the short, fat troll leaped out from under the trees and raced toward him. As they drew even with each other, the big troll tossed the mayor's wife into the air, and the second troll caught her, then tucked her under his own hairy arm and charged down the road. The mayor's wife could only squeak as she bounced along. The two trolls ran up and down the road, tossing her back and forth each time they passed. The trolls were so big and so nasty that no one knew where to turn. Who was big enough to fight with the trolls?

Then Ivy had a thought. She'd heard the mayor say that he'd better not see any more magical creatures. She knew that the whole town wanted them to go away too. And she knew that the queen must be watching from her coach. But there was only one way to stop the trolls. Ivy raced out through the back door and up to Cedric's nest.

"Cedric!" Ivy cried as she reached the huge nest behind the house. "Oh, Cedric! We need your help! There are trolls on the loose! They've got the mayor's wife! Hurry!"

Cedric poked his head up and squawked loudly. "Trolls, you say? Griffins hate trolls! Where are the trolls? Where?" Poof began to bark. Ivy ran on down the path to the stream, calling to Balthazar. Cedric took off into the air while Poof ran straight to the hazel trees and yapped frantically at the trolls who were still hiding there.

The last two trolls leaped out. The tall, thin one grabbed Poof, tucked him under his arm, and sprinted down the road after the first two trolls. The big-nosed troll charged after him with a grunt, which meant, "Wait for me! I saw him first!" Then all four trolls circled around, flinging Poof and Mistress Peevish high in the air, catching them, and tossing them back up again, like jugglers. They did it again and again.

Flying overhead, Cedric dove toward the big-nosed troll, who had Poof. "I GUARD THE POOF!" he crowed, and grabbed the troll's shoulders with his strong, eagle-like claws. The troll dropped Poof, but the short, fat troll snatched him up and ran in the other direction.

As the griffin turned to chase after the troll, Ivy and Balthazar arrived. The dragon watched while the short, fat troll and the biggest troll raced along the road flinging Poof and the mayor's wife back and forth to each other. Some of the villagers ran this way and that, while others were frozen in terror.

"This is bad," confirmed Balthazar.

"What?" asked Ivy.

"They are playig an old troll gabe. It's called four-man whumpus. We've got to stop theb before they reach the goal!"

CHAPTER 13

Snatched!

"**W**here is the goal?" Ivy asked the dragon.

"I can't tell yet," answered Balthazar, "but they usually use subthig big and shidy."

Ivy looked around. The biggest, shiniest thing she could see was the royal coach. A prickle of fear went up her back.

"Then what will they do?" Ivy asked hastily. "What are the rules of four-man whumpus?"

"There are no rules. They just cause as much

trouble as they can, and then they throw whatever they are using for a ball down at the goal
and WHUMP it very hard."

Ivy watched helplessly as Poof was tossed
again from one troll to the next. Meanwhile,
Cedric was perched on the biggest troll's shoulders, pecking its head with his beak. "Can't
you stop them?" cried Ivy.

"I'm an old dragon, and not as fast as I used
to be, but I will try!" Balthazar charged into
the road, breathing fire. The trolls looked up
at him in surprise, then made vile noises at him
and went back to playing their game, wilder and
faster than before. When the big-nosed troll
looped around, juggling Poof from one hand
to the other, the griffin flapped his huge wings
in the troll's face. The troll dropped Poof on
the ground, where the tiny dog immediately
nipped his ankles. Balthazar let loose a flame
and toasted the troll's backside. "YOWIE!"

shrieked the troll as he scrambled away down the road with smoke coming from his tail.

Before the dragon could catch his breath, another troll swooped down and snatched Poof up again, hurling the little dog high in the air. As the three remaining trolls raced around juggling their bundles back and forth, the dragon and the griffin circled them carefully. They had to get the trolls without hurting Poof or the mayor's wife.

Ivy could hardly stand to watch. There had to be something else she could do, some way to help, but she was afraid she was just too little. Little . . . Suddenly she had an idea. Pixies! They were the littlest people of all, but they had managed to chase the neighbors away the day before, and they had bothered Peter almost to the point of tears when she told them to attack him this morning. Would they fight the trolls if she asked them?

Ivy ran to the back of the garden and stood under the apple tree where the pixies were staying. "Pixies, HELP!" she cried. "It's a troll attack! Please, come and help us! They've got Poof!"

A loud buzzing could be heard from the branches of the tree. All at once, the pixies swarmed around her, some of them clinging to her clothing and hair. Ivy laughed. "Thank you! All of you! This way!" Ivy reached the road just in time to see Poof squirm out of the short, fat troll's grasp, leap to the ground, and run straight toward her while the biggest troll was busy twirling the mayor's wife like a baton.

Ivy reached for Poof, but the next thing she knew, she herself was being tossed up in the air and caught by the tall, thin troll. He tucked her under his smelly armpit and circled back up the road. "YUCK!" yelled Ivy as she bounced up and down. "OH YUCK!"

Suddenly, the short, fat troll ran up to them and made a grab for Ivy. He got her by one arm, but the tall troll wouldn't let go of her leg. Ivy thought she might be split in two as the two trolls played tug-of-war with her, poking and punching one another with their free hands.

"PIXIES, TO ME! TO ME!" yelled Ivy. In an instant, the air was thick with furious pixies on the attack. They bit the trolls' ears, poked them in their noses, and pulled their hair. They even pulled their eyelashes. "YOW! YOW! YOWIE!" shrieked the trolls, but still they held on to Ivy.

Out of the corner of her eye, Ivy could see Poof, brave little Poof, yapping at the two fighting trolls and nipping at their heels. The pixies buzzed in fast circles around the trolls' heads to make them dizzy. Finally both trolls dropped Ivy in the dirt. The short, fat troll pulled Poof from his leg and threw him up in the air. The tall, thin troll ran away, slapping himself and squealing something *very* nasty at the pixies, who chased him down the road.

Only two trolls remained. Balthazar was looking for a safe way to breathe fire at them, but now the biggest troll had Poof and the short, fat troll had the mayor's wife. He didn't want to scorch them by accident.

Suddenly the dragon felt a big sneeze coming on. "AH-AH-AH-*CHOOO*!" he sneezed, right at the troll who had the mayor's wife. The troll dropped her like a boulder. He just stood there for a moment next to the grand and haughty Mistress Peevish, both of them covered with smoke and dragon snot. Then he fled down the road after the other trolls.

Now only the biggest troll was left. He held Poof tightly in one raised hand, and he was charging straight for the royal coach. He was still playing the game . . . and it was clear that the queen's coach was the goal! When the coachmen saw him coming, their eyes grew wide. They struggled to control the two snow-white horses, who were rearing and stomping in terror.

Ivy watched in horror as the troll bounded far ahead of Cedric and Balthazar with Poof held high over his head. Just when it seemed the little dog was doomed to be whumped, Poof sunk his sharp teeth into the troll's finger and bit down hard.

The troll roared and tried to shake Poof loose, but Poof only bit down harder. He held on until the troll gave one last, powerful shake, which sent the little dog flying. Poof fell to the ground and lay still.

"Poof! Oh no!" cried Ivy. Then Poof jumped to his feet and shook himself all over.

"I GUARD THE POOF!" bellowed Cedric

as he dove for the tiny dog. The griffin picked him up ever so gently in his talons and flew him away to safety while Balthazar let loose a fiery breath at the headstrong troll. The troll just howled in anger. He rammed the royal coach and whumped on it with his fists until one mighty blast from the dragon sizzled his fur from head to foot. With that, the troll leaped straight into the air and hit the ground running. Ivy watched as he disappeared around a bend in the road, making a high-pitched squeal that meant he was calling for his mother.

For a moment, there was complete silence. The royal carriage was scorched on one corner and dented at the top. Then from inside the carriage there came a sound . . . a sound like someone crying.

Ivy felt terrible. What if they had made the new queen cry?

CHAPTER 14

The New Queen

There was a light knocking coming from inside the carriage. One of the coachmen climbed down and opened the door. "Make way for Her Majesty, Queen Emmeline!" he proclaimed. He lowered the coach steps and out climbed a girl, pausing on the top step. She was not much bigger than Ivy, but she wore a jeweled crown, two sizes too big, and a long fur-trimmed robe. And she wasn't crying at all. She was laughing and laughing as if she would never stop.

Ivy was so surprised she almost forgot to curtsy. She could feel her own mouth turning up at the corners. And then she couldn't help herself. She broke out laughing too. Then Peter began to laugh, and Grandmother. Soon Mayor Peevish and the town council decided that if the *queen* was laughing, *they* had better laugh too. Before long the whole crowd was laughing, and the little queen laughed so hard she hiccuped.

When the laughter finally quieted, the queen came down the coach steps. She straightened her crown, then said, "I'd very much like to meet the dragon, and the griffin, and the girl who fought the trolls."

Grandmother put her hand on Ivy's shoulder. "Go up and introduce yourself, dear," she whispered. Ivy felt suddenly shy, but she did as

Grandmother said. She approached the queen
and curtsied again, then motioned for the griffin and the dragon to join her.

"Your Majesty," she said, "I'd like to present
the dragon, who is called Balthazar, and the
griffin, who is called Cedric." The dragon and
the griffin each gave a low bow.

"And who are you?" asked the little queen.

"My name is Ivy, and I live in this cottage, and these are my friends. They're magical creatures. Everyone else said they had to go. They said magical creatures cause too much trouble. But my grandmother said they could stay."

"I'm glad they stayed," said the queen. "And who owns the little white dog? He was so brave fighting the trolls!" The grand and haughty Mistress Peevish, slightly scorched, pushed her way forward to the queen. "He's mine!" she cried, wiping some dragon goo off her cheek. Her dress was black at the edges, and she still smelled of smoke. "This griffin creature has been keeping him from me!"

"Is this true?" the queen asked Ivy.

"I think the truth is that Poof may not want to go home," said Ivy. "He and the griffin have become friends."

As if to prove her right, Poof stuck his head

out from under the griffin's wing, where he had been hiding. He yapped several times and dove back under.

"I see," said the young queen thoughtfully. "Call the little dog forth, please."

Mistress Peevish called to him, but Poof wouldn't come. Then Ivy called, and Poof slowly crept out and sat by her feet.

Queen Emmeline touched him with her scepter. "As a reward for great bravery against trolls, I declare that from this day forward this dog, known as Poof, is a free dog. He belongs to himself, and he can make his home wherever he pleases."

Ivy smiled to herself. She liked this queen already. The queen turned to the mayor's wife and said, "I shall arrange for you to have a new dog. You may go."

Mistress Peevish looked as if she wanted to object, but she curtsied and said, "As you wish, Your Majesty."

Suddenly there was a buzzing around their heads. The pixies wanted some attention too. The little queen waved her scepter in the air. "OUCH!" she cried. "Something pinched me!" She dropped the scepter and swatted the air with both hands.

"Your Majesty, if you please, I can help," offered Ivy.

"Yes!" exclaimed the queen. "Help!"

Ivy took both of the queen's hands in hers and explained about the tiny winged people, and that she mustn't swat them. She showed her how to hold her hand out and talk nicely to them. Soon an itty-bitty pixie girl came to land on the queen's open hand and gave a curtsy. The queen gasped in delight. Her eyes lit up.

"Oh, she's perfect!" the queen cried. "And she likes me!" More pixies came and settled on her shoulders, and some sat on her crown. The queen smiled a great big smile. Then she looked serious. She cleared her throat and climbed to the top of the carriage steps again so that everyone could see her.

"My people," she began, "I have traveled the kingdom far and wide, through one lovely village after another. And now I have come to Broomsweep, the last village. There was no one to greet me in the town square. Instead, I found that the village was overrun by horrible trolls. My own coach was scorched and whumped and dented while you, my people, were in chaos. And after going to so many perfect towns, I have come to an inescapable conclusion."

Everyone inhaled a big breath and held it, waiting to hear what she would say. Mayor Peevish and the whole town council and all the others stood there with their mouths hanging open, and Mistress Peevish looked as if she might faint.

"I declare Broomsweep to be the most perfect, most unique, most fun of any town in the kingdom of Evermore!" cried the queen. "It is the BEST town of all!"

CHAPTER 15

Ivy's Dream

A roar went up from the crowd. People threw their hats in the air and cheered. The neighbors gathered around Grandmother and Ivy, and all tried to pat their backs at the same time.

Grandmother just smiled. "I told you things would work out!" she said happily.

Then Grandmother invited the queen in for tea, and also the queen's nanny, who had been waiting in the coach. They were both pleased to accept the invitation. Queen Emmeline left her robe and her crown and her scepter in the carriage. "This cottage—it's different from all the others," she marveled. "And what a big, splendid garden! It must be fun to play in."

As soon as they were finished with tea, Ivy took the queen around the garden and showed her each of the creatures staying there. The foxes let Queen Emmeline scratch them behind their ears just the way Ivy did. So did the beaver and the chipmunk. Queen Emmeline had a gentle touch, and she wasn't afraid at all. She even fed a worm to the robin. Then they had a long visit with Balthazar and Cedric, and played with the pixies. By the time the afternoon was over, Ivy and Queen Emmeline were fast friends.

The next day, the royal fair came to town. Colorful tents went up in the village square. Dancers danced, minstrels sang, and jugglers juggled. There was a sword swallower and a tightrope walker. A jester told funny stories and jokes. A magician did fantastic tricks.

When it came time for the royal joust, Queen Emmeline asked Ivy to sit with her to watch. Ivy asked if Peter could join them too. The three of them watched as two knights in shining armor tried to knock each other off their horses with their jousting lances.

Broomsweep had never seen anything to compare with this. It was the finest fair the villagers could have imagined.

Ivy only wished for one thing more. She had waited before asking so Cedric would have plenty of time to practice his landings. Now she took him aside and nervously said, "I have something to ask you."

"Ask anything!" Cedric replied. "*Aawk—* griffins aim to please."

"Well then, would you, could you, take me flying?" Ivy asked.

"C. T. L. Griffin, high flyer, at your service!" Cedric answered, holding his head up proudly and puffing out his chest.

Ivy turned to the dragon. "If you're feeling better, Balthazar, would you please take Queen Emmeline flying too?"

"I should be honored," said the dragon.

"But is it quite safe?" asked Queen Emmeline's nanny.

"Why, of course," said Grandmother. "There is nothing safer than riding on a magical creature."

Finally the nanny agreed. Grandmother bundled the girls up in warm cloaks, and the queen's footmen boosted them onto the creatures' backs.

Ivy clutched Cedric tightly around the neck. She felt him crouch, gathering his powerful muscles. With a sudden leap, they were airborne, the dragon only a heartbeat behind. Ivy watched in wonder as the ground fell away and they rose above the treetops. A flock of birds scattered around them, and Ivy felt like a bird herself.

"Higher!" she cried, and the griffin pumped his mighty wings faster. The dragon's wings flapped harder too. Queen Emmeline laughed.

"Higher!" the queen cried, until the cottages below them were as small as acorns. Ivy could see clear across the valley and the green spread of forest next to her grandmother's cottage, all the way to the distant blue mountains. As they climbed nearer to the clouds, Ivy looked down at the town and stretched one hand toward it. The whole village of Broomsweep seemed to fit in the palm of her hand.

They hovered for a time, then coasted downward in slow circles, taking in the view. Finally they floated over the village square. Ivy could see the villagers' faces looking up at them. Everyone was waving and cheering. It was even better than her dream. At last Cedric drifted down to earth in a perfect landing, and Balthazar after him.

It was time for Queen Emmeline to go. She said goodbye to Balthazar and Cedric. She thanked Grandmother for sharing her marvelous garden and gave Ivy a warm embrace. Then she and her nanny got into the dented golden coach and rode away, with Queen Emmeline waving her hand out the window.

After that day, things changed in the village of Broomsweep. It was still a clean town, but hardly anybody swept their front steps twice a day anymore. They were too busy with other things. James the Shoemaker was teaching himself to juggle. Bess the Candlemaker was learning some ballads to sing. And Jacob the

Baker was practicing his favorite jokes on anyone who would listen. After all, Broomsweep had been declared the most *fun* town in the kingdom, and the villagers intended to keep it that way.

Since the day Queen Emmeline chose Broomsweep as the best town, the villagers had changed their minds about magical creatures too. They even put up a sign in the village square. It said MAGICAL CREATURES WELCOME.

Of course, the grand and haughty Mistress Peevish stayed just as bossy as ever. Her new dog looked a lot like Poof, only with golden-colored fur. She named her Foof. And as often as not, when Ivy went out to do her morning chores, there would be Foof, hiding under the lilies.

Edwina and Marta, who used to tease Ivy, came to her now to ask if she would teach them how to befriend the pixies. So she did. Peter helped her. Ivy was so happy that she decided to forget about their teasing. Now all the children were allowed to play with her, no matter how dirty they got.

And so Ivy went on working and playing in Grandmother's garden, doing her very best to live happily ever after, while waiting to see what magical creature would arrive next.